Telescope Troubles

by
Nate Ball

illustrated by
Macky Pamintuan

HARPER
An Imprint of HarperCollins*Publishers*

Alien in My Pocket: Telescope Troubles
Text by Nate Ball, copyright © 2016 by HarperCollins Publishers
Illustrations by Macky Pamintuan, copyright © 2016 by HarperCollins Publishers
For information address HarperCollins Children's Books, a division of HarperCollins
Publishers, 195 Broadway, New York, NY 10007.
Library of Congress catalog card number: 2015005994
ISBN 978-0-06-237089-1 (trade bdg.)—ISBN 978-0-06-237088-4 (pbk.)
Typography by Sean Boggs
15 16 17 18 19 LP/RRDH   10 9 8 7 6 5 4 3 2 1
❖
First Edition

Contents

Brain Dump

Okay, I'm just going admit something right from the start: I've had an alien no bigger than a soda can secretly hiding in my bedroom for the last few months.

You might think that it'd be an amazing thrill—but you'd be mistaken.

I've seen and done things that nobody in human history ever has. I started a citywide panic and successfully launched a spaceship into orbit out of my own backyard, and I created an electromagnet strong enough to nearly destroy a city building—all to prevent an alien invasion of planet Earth.

It's been a pretty hectic and stressful few months.

And to be perfectly honest, it's been a lot for a fourth-grader to handle.

I've had trouble sleeping. My grades have suffered. I dislocated my shoulder. It still clicks when I raise my hand. I had to erase my little brother's short-term memory, and now he seems weirder than ever. I almost got eaten alive by a pack of bears. Oh, and I've had to smuggle about four hundred tons of Ritz Crackers and SweeTarts into my room. Amp, my houseguest from the planet Erde, has some odd ideas about food and nutrition.

My parents are convinced I have mental issues, because they often catch me talking, laughing, and arguing in my room—and they think I'm alone! Mom's even taken me to Dr. Bell's office twice now for "a chat," but he just told her that I was sleepy and slightly confused, but an otherwise perfectly ordinary kid.

If he only knew . . .

There have also been a few more unexpected side effects caused by playing host to an alien. For example, actually knowing a real-life alien totally ruins every movie you see about aliens! And it changes the way you think about Earth: we are *so* not the center of the universe. Most important, it

3

answers the age-old question about whether life exists on other planets—it does, and I have the roommate to prove it.

All this makes evenings like tonight extra special.

See, tonight is my night off. Amp is hanging out with Olivia, my next-door neighbor, classmate, best friend, and the only other person on the planet who knows about the alien hiding out in the McGees' house.

Twice a week Olivia babysits Amp. Or, more accurately, she prevents him from starting a worldwide panic while I get some quality alone time.

What do I do while he's away? These blissful few hours of peace and quiet are often spent cleaning my room—Amp makes a serious mess. Ritz Cracker crumbs are everywhere. He eats them like a termite eats wood. Sometimes I nap. Sometimes I just stare at the wall and let my brain relax. Like I said, hiding an alien from your parents and little brother can be pretty mentally exhausting.

As the sun dips below the garage roof outside

my second-story bedroom window, I fall into a herky-jerky sleep, dreaming about eating a salami-and-worm sandwich in front of my class—it's my brain's favorite weird dream and one I've actually grown to enjoy.

Of course, that nap was the beginning of the end of Amp's time here on Earth.

This is the story of how I let my guard down and how my nosy little brother stepped in and the world as we know it nearly ended.

Meltdown

pparently, I didn't feel the first few Milk Duds bounce off my face.

It wasn't my fault. I was sound asleep.

Then one of the chocolate candies hit me square on the front tooth with a loud *click*. I sat up like startled cat.

I blinked in the dim light, trying to make sense of what had hit me.

I picked up the Milk Dud in question and stared at it like it was a bullet from another universe. I put a finger to my tooth and gave it a wiggle to see if the flying candy had knocked it loose.

My sheets, blankets, and pillow were covered with about forty Milk Duds. I popped one in my mouth and started chewing slowly.

Another candy zipped through the dim light

out of nowhere. I was slow to duck—and blink. It beaned me square in the open eye.

"Ouch!" I shouted, pressing a palm to my stinging, watering eye.

I scrambled to the window. The flying candies were coming through the big hole in my window screen. I could see Olivia down in my backyard, eating from and holding the biggest box of Milk Duds I had ever seen.

"Why are you throwing Milk Duds at my face?" I hissed. "You almost blinded me!"

"I called, but your mom told me your doctor says you need to sleep more. She said you might have a sleeping disorder."

"I do," I said. "His name is Amp!"

The night sky was sparkling with stars. The little bulb by our back door was on, so I could see Olivia well enough to know something was on her mind.

"What do you want?" I asked. "You're supposed to be babysitting till eleven thirty. Is it eleven thirty already?"

She pushed a wad of half-chewed Milk Duds to the side of her mouth with her tongue. She now looked like a distracted squirrel. "Something happened," she said from the other side of her mouth.

I stared down at her. "Something? Can you be more specific?"

"Something bad."

"How bad?" I said, shaking my head.

She paused, swallowed the gob of chocolate with some effort, and then looked around as if she were trying to figure out how to tell me the news. She sighed. "Amp kinda had a meltdown."

"What kind of meltdown? I didn't think aliens could even have meltdowns."

"I didn't think so either."

"Then what do you mean he had a meltdown?"

9

"It's like his spirit was broken."

I grabbed a fistful of my hair in frustration. "What does that mean?" I growled. "Olivia, what's wrong with you? First you almost knock my tooth out, then you nearly blind me, then you get all mysterious."

"Sorry," she said, blinking. Now she really did seem upset. She held up the box of candy. "I'm an emotional eater."

"Okay," I said. "Take it easy. Just relax. He drives me crazy, too. Where is Amp now?"

"I don't know."

"Is he nearby?"

"I don't know."

"Did he come back to my house?"

"I don't know."

"Which direction did he go?"

"I don't know."

"Was he going to get something?"

"I. Don't. Know."

"You're some babysitter! I hope you're not expecting a tip!"

Olivia looked down at her shoes. I thought she might start to cry.

"Okay," I said. "We'll figure this out. He gets touchy sometimes. When did this all happen?"

"About two hours ago."

"*What?* He's got a two-hour lead? He can't be out on his own! He can't be seen. He'll get eaten by a cat or a badger."

"I know that!" she shouted.

"Shhh! My parents . . . Why didn't you come get me earlier?"

"I told you, I tried! Your mom has you in sleepy-time lockdown. I was trying to find him on my own so you could get your beauty rest."

I thought for a moment. "Okay, go get your grandpa's ladder. My mom is not going to let me out, not at this hour. We'll find him together."

Olivia nodded and walked off, looking relieved to have the beginnings of a plan, any plan, taking shape.

"And save some Milk Duds for me," I said, trying to make the situation less tense. I'm not sure if it worked. Olivia didn't look back. She disappeared into the hole in the fence between our two backyards.

I popped my screen out and dropped it into

the bushes below. I looked around my room. An uneasy feeling overtook me. I quietly closed my door all the way. I could hear my parents talking excitedly down in the kitchen.

I turned back to my empty room. "Somebody remind me to strangle that alien when I get my hands on him." And then I heard the ladder rattle against the side of the house and I climbed out to go save Amp—again.

03

Scope It Out

"**W**hoa, this telescope is almost as big as a canoe."

Olivia nodded. "Amp said exactly the same thing. I happened to mention that my grandpa used to be into astronomy when my grandma was alive. They used to stand out here at night and look at stars and stuff. It was their hobby."

If Amp were here, he'd so say:

"Council Note: Astronomy is the study of celestial objects such as stars, planets, moons, and galaxies. Earthlings have primitive equipment for their study. They call them telescopes and they use them to stare at the sky."

13

Amp had been recording messages for his home planet since the day he came to Earth. Usually it annoyed me, but at that moment, I actually really missed the little guy.

It was nearing midnight now, and the surrounding homes were dark and quiet. The air was filled with the noise of crickets and the hoot of an owl that lived somewhere nearby. Apparently, Olivia's grandpa was upstairs in bed. We had to be careful and quiet—though her grandfather snored like a bear, so we'd have plenty of warning if we woke him.

I poked my eye into the eyehole thingy, but I couldn't really see anything. I started to turn nobs, move a slider back and forth, and pull some levers. "This is right up Amp's alley."

"Tell me about it." Olivia sighed. "When he heard it was stored in the garage, he insisted we haul it out and set it up."

"Sounds like him. How does this thing even work?"

"I have no idea," Olivia said quietly.

I walked around the impressive-looking piece of equipment and whistled. "This must be worth a lot of money."

"Maybe," Olivia said with a shrug. "Grandpa never takes it out anymore. I wish I hadn't mentioned it to Amp."

Olivia had set up the telescope in the center of her backyard and had pointed it up toward the heavens. The grass under my bare feet felt damp and cold. I looked around the perfectly still backyard.

"Amp?" I said louder than I should have. "Knock it off. Let's go. I have to sleep and so does Olivia."

Olivia shook her head. "It won't work. He's gone. I can feel it in my bones. He freaked out."

"What do you mean he's gone? Where would he go?"

She didn't answer, but I could see her shrug again.

"Okay, so tell me again exactly what happened."

"It was so weird. He was doing calculations in his head. Charting the stars. He was totally excited. He was sure he was going to find his home planet, Erde. Or not exactly his planet—his sun, the one Erde goes around. He said it would look like the tiniest blue star from here. I thought he was going to pass out from excitement."

"Yeah," I said. "That sounds like him."

"But it was taking him forever. After, like, an hour of nothing, I got bored and zonked out on the couch in the garage. I kept hearing him talking to himself. Clapping his little hands. Jumping up and down on this stepladder I gave him to stand on."

"Yeah . . ."

"Then . . . I don't know. He found it—his sun or whatever. I heard him shouting about it. He woke me up. I came out here. And then he got real quiet."

"Why?"

"He said something about a flash. Some mysterious light. I don't know. He said something had happened to his planet."

"Really?" I whispered, and sat down on the small stepladder.

"He said it had blown up. Or exploded. Or something."

"Oh."

"Then he got mad at the telescope because it wasn't powerful enough. He got crazy. He was ranting and raving. He said his planet was gone. All was lost. He was the only Erdian left in the universe. Blah, blah, blah."

"Man."

"He said he was giving himself up. There was no point to anything anymore. No point in hiding. 'It's all over,' he kept repeating."

"Wow. What a freak-out. I wouldn't worry too much. He's just overreacting—again. He's

17

always pushy and bossy and acts like a know-it-all, but most of the time he doesn't know what he's talking about."

"Well, now he's overreacting to the point that he's run off and given up."

"Whatever," I said.

"No, he was serious. That's what I meant when I said his spirit was broken. He was like a different person. He even said good-bye."

"He said good-bye? Good grief."

"I never thought it would end like this," Olivia said with a sniff.

I could tell Olivia had really started to cry, but I didn't want to make a big deal out of it. I was more irritated than anything else. Amp could be an emotional wrecking ball. He could mess up your life in ways that you never thought possible.

"Go to bed," I said. "Don't worry. He'll come around. Don't take anything he says too seriously. He'll drive you crazy. I'll go back my room, see if I can contact him with brain waves, or whatever we call it. I'm sure everything will be all right."

"I'm glad you think so," Olivia whispered. She gave me a little wave in the dark, then turned and went into her house without looking back.

I was left alone, surrounded by the noises of the night, feeling the damp grass quickly making my feet feel cold.

"You're in big trouble, mister," I said to the surrounding darkness.

04

Answering the Call

I climbed up the ladder still leaning against my house and crawled back into my room like a thief in the night.

I quietly opened my bedroom door and listened, but there was no sound coming from downstairs. The lights were all out. I looked down the hall, and the only light I could see was leaking out from under Taylor's bedroom door. This was late for him. I considered seeing what he was up to, but I had my own problems to deal with.

I collapsed onto my bed with a moan.

I thought of Olivia crying in the darkness but pushed it out of my mind. I had never seen her cry before.

Amp could make a mess as easily as most people could make toast.

I balled my hands into fists. I wondered if I was the first fourth-grader in the history of Reed School to suffer from high blood pressure.

I was tired and grumpy and sleepy and frustrated. It was the middle of the night. And I realized I'd felt this way pretty much since Amp flew through my window screen and crash-landed his football-size spaceship onto my bed.

Talk about turning a kid's life inside out.

Yes, it was fun to hear about life on other planets and to learn about space travel. We'd had some pretty interesting adventures. And I'll admit, there was something exciting about hiding the greatest secret ever from the rest of the world—except for Olivia, of course.

But that was the thing. I couldn't discuss Amp with anyone but Olivia. Even my parents were clueless. I had to keep this incredible secret all bottled up inside, and sometimes the pressure of it made me feel like a human volcano.

The sad truth was that I knew Amp would be taken away from me the instant that word got out I was hiding an alien in my pocket. The police or the government or the army would swoop in, put him in cage, and rush him away to some top secret laboratory to poke and probe and experiment on him like a frog in a middle-school biology class.

The news would cause a freak-out on a global scale.

And the fact that he was a military scout from the planet Erde visiting Earth to scope out a future Erdian invasion would not have sat well with the army types.

The thought of millions of pint-size Smurf-looking aliens trying to take over was hard to imagine, even for me, but it wasn't hard to imagine it would be a big mess for both sides.

Luckily we had put a stop to the whole invasion-of-Earth business.

Amp's boss—his name was Ohm—had shown up one day, and then had returned to Erde to report that Earth was not suitable for a take-over. For one, humans—and everything else on Earth—turned out to be much bigger than the Erdians had thought. Their estimates were way off. And experience had taught the Erdians that it was better to pick on someone their own size.

23

Plus, humans were clever, bossy, and very unpredictable, and we owned cats—all bad traits for an Erdian enemy.

My Amp memories now fluttered through my mind like a thousand little blue headaches.

"Amp?" I called out silently with my mind as I stared up at my ceiling. "Can you hear me? Come back, and we'll figure this out together."

Amp and I could communicate using our minds. But it really wasn't a very pleasant experience—Olivia said it gave her the willies. To me it was sort of like pouring cold butterscotch pudding through both your earholes at the same time.

I lay on my bed, nagging at him with my mind for ten minutes straight. Finally I must have worn him down, because he answered in the saddest, most defeated voice I had ever heard.

"It's over, Zack. I give up. All is lost. I'm the last Erdian."

I gasped and sat up on the edge of my bed. I closed my eyes, pressed a finger to each of my temples, and focused my mind. "Relax, little man. Snap out of it. You don't know anything for sure. Like I said, come back, and we'll figure this out."

"No, Zack, I'm finished. Thank you for being my host, for being my friend, but a good Erdian scout knows when his mission has failed. I just don't care anymore. This is Erdian Scout Amp, over and out."

"Wait! Amp? Get your blue butt back here this instant."

There was no response. Just eerie silence.

My eyes watered, and I blinked away the moisture. I looked out my window and knew our conversation had a silver lining: He was nearby. Our ability to speak with our minds had a limited range, maybe fifty yards max. So he was

25

somewhere within half a football field of me. There was still hope. I might not be able to find him, but at least I knew he was close enough that when he was ready to stop acting crazy, he would come home.

I sighed and collapsed back onto my bed. I could feel my brain easing into sleep out of exhaustion or confusion or just plain old frustration.

He'd come around. He'd get the munchies and come crawling back for his SweeTarts, Ritz Crackers, and sunflower seeds. He'd apologize. We'd watch one of his favorite old-time horror movies, like *The Wolf Man* or *The Mummy*.

Everything would be all right.

As I drifted off to sleep, I had no idea how wrong I was.

05

The Cat Gets Out

My first thought when I woke up wasn't about Amp or his meltdown or his disappearance.

It was about pancakes.

I was starving. And Saturday morning meant blueberry pancakes, crisp bacon, buttery biscuits, and sweet pineapple juice. Mom pulled out all the stops on Saturday mornings.

To be honest, I had forgotten about Amp and simply let my grumbling stomach lead the way. I rumbled down the stairs, my hair bouncing like a rooster tail, and I still had on the clothes I had been wearing last night.

I didn't realize anything was amiss till I plopped down in my regular chair. The air wasn't filled with the familiar smells of freshly brewed coffee and steamy pancakes; instead the kitchen was deserted, except for Mr. Jinxy, our family cat, who sat on the kitchen counter and stared at me suspiciously with squinty eyes.

No juice pouring. No biscuits baking. No bacon sizzling.

My fantasies of a full stomach came to a screeching halt.

I glanced around. "Now what?"

My parents and Aunt Joni looked over when I poked my head into the living room. They all seemed deeply concerned and highly irritated.

"Hi, Aunt Joni. What are you doing here? Are you taking us out for breakfast?" I asked hopefully.

"See? That's what I'm talking about!" Aunt Joni exclaimed to my parents, jabbing her pointing finger in my direction.

"What do you know about this?" Dad asked, waving around a piece of binder paper.

"About what?" I asked, confused.

"It's about your brother running off," Mom said. "And his crazy talk."

"Oh, he always talks crazy," I said with a shrug. "Why did he run off this time?"

The three of them gave me disapproving looks. I stuffed my hands into my pockets, not exactly sure of the situation I had walked into.

My mother powered up her cell phone to call the neighbors to see if they'd seen Taylor. My father was looking for his car keys. He was going to see if he could find Taylor himself. And my aunt just sat there and stared daggers at me. I was never so glad to hear the kitchen phone ring in my whole life.

I backed out of the living room and lifted the phone off its wall-mounted cradle before it could ring a second time.

"Uh . . . hello?" I said. My stomach growled painfully at the same time.

"Is this Taylor McGee?" a strange man asked in a pushy voice.

"No, it's not. I'm his brother, Zack. Zack McGee. Who is this?"

"Is he there? He's late for our meeting."

"Meeting? What meeting? He's only in the second grade. Second-graders don't have meetings."

"I was promised an exclusive."

"I'm not even sure what that means."

"We had a deal," he said, sounding irritated. "There's already a crowd here. Does he have a cell phone? Can you give me his mobile number?"

"No, I can't. Because he doesn't have a cell phone. I don't have one either, and I'm older than he is." I paused. "I'm sorry, you never said who you are."

"Who is that, Zack?" Dad barked from the living room.

"Hold on a second!" I called out.

"Listen, pal, my editor is all over me. Just tell me how I can reach Taylor McGee?"

"Mister, are you sure you're calling—"

Just then the phone clicked twice, meaning we had another incoming call. "Uh, hold on," I said. I quickly pressed the Talk button, switching over to the other line. "Hello?"

"Is this Taylor?" another man's voice asked immediately.

"Seriously?" I said, pulling the phone away from my head to look at it briefly.

"Zack?" the deep voice said.

"Who in the heck is—"

"This is Mr. Prentiss. Remember, we met when you won your school's science fair with your magnificent battery-powered magnet? I was one of the judges. My company sponsored your school's science fair."

"Oh, sure. How's it going?" I grabbed my face and squeezed it in embarrassment.

Mr. Prentiss was indeed a big shot in my town. He was a scientist and inventor with his own engineering company. He had wanted to give me a summer job after I won my school's science fair, but I avoided his calls until he gave up. It was really Amp who had won that science fair. I had just gotten the credit for Amp's work. Honestly, Taylor was the science genius in our family, but I had stolen a lot of his thunder with that magnet. And I hadn't let him forget it.

"Your brother's started quite a kerfuffle."

"Kerfluff-what? Hold on a second, Mr. Prentiss. I have someone on the other line."

I pressed my hand to the phone. "Hey, you guys, there's a phone call for Taylor. . . ."

"What is *wrong* with you?" my aunt Joni asked.

I made a painful smile. "I don't know. I'm pretty hungry and slightly dizzy."

"Are you even paying attention to the events going on around you right now, Zack?" Dad growled at me as he grabbed the phone away.

"Uh . . ." I replied. "Sort of . . ."

"We've got a family emergency here," Mom snapped. "Stop goofing around on the phone and help us sort this out. Gosh!"

That was when I saw it. There was a sheet of binder paper on the coffee table. It was a note written in red colored pencil in Taylor's unmistakable fat lettering.

Dear Mom and Dad,
Good morning. I have made the scientific discovery of the century. I have proof of alien life. In fact, I have an actual alien. He's small, blue, and funny-looking. I named him Buddy. I have called a press conference and will announce my discovery

to the world this morning. Make sure the TV is on and you can see me. I didn't tell you because I knew you wouldn't let me. Sorry. I will probably become superfamous, so just letting you know before things get out of hand. I'll call later.

Your son,

Taylor Q. McGee

P.S. Tell Zack I'll let him hold the alien if he wants.

I dropped the note, and it floated to the ground like a dry leaf.

In an instant my world had collapsed around me, like I had just been sucked into a black hole.

My worst nightmare—and the thing I had worked tirelessly to prevent for months—had just come true.

Taylor had discovered Amp and was going to tell the world.

06

Seeing the Light

I stood in my room in such a state of shock, I couldn't move.

I was struck dumb—I had never really known what it meant until that moment.

I had no plan. I had no ideas. I had no hope of stopping the events that were spiraling out of my control.

Amp was right: All was lost.

That was when I heard the beeping.

At first I thought I was hearing something inside my head, like alarm bells warning me that I was about to faint.

But that wasn't it.

The sound was muffled, high-pitched, and urgent. And extremely annoying.

I shook my head. I followed the noise past my

bed and my desk and into my dark closet. I flipped on the light and listened.

Without thinking, I slowly pulled the wool blanket off Amp's broken spaceship.

There, on the side of the spaceship, somehow glowing through the spaceship's shiny metal, was a blinking purple light.

I gasped. The noise was loud and annoying, and the light was unmistakably purple. And I knew what that meant.

Amp had once explained that the appearance of a purple light on the side of his ship meant the Erdian invasion of Earth had begun.

My messy closet seemed to spin.

Amp's planet hadn't come to some terrible, sudden end. It hadn't exploded. The light he saw was probably the launch of the attack, one million tiny football-size spaceships shooting through a hole in space and time, taking the Erdian shortcut to Earth.

I stumbled out of my closet, clutching at the pain in my empty stomach.

If the attack was on, that meant something had happened to Amp's boss, Ohm. Ohm had blasted off back to Erde right from my own backyard to cancel the invasion. He knew that humans were too big for the Erdians to defeat. So what happened? Did he take a wrong turn at Saturn? Did he get lost traveling through time and end up a million years from now? A hundred questions swirled through the space between my ears.

All I could think then was that I had to tell Olivia. She was the only person who would understand. She would figure out what we had to do, who to tell, how to get the warning out about the Erdians who would soon arrive to attack our planet. She was good in an emergency. I was not.

I looked out my window to see if Olivia was in her backyard, but movement in my own backyard caught my eye.

Behind the side door of our garage, the one a few feet from the gate in our backyard fence, I saw a bike wheel peeking out. The wheel rocked back and forth a bit, as if someone were struggling with it. I leaned forward and focused.

It looked like my mom's bike. Had I just caught a bike thief with truly terrible timing?

With an invisible shove, the whole front wheel and handlebars emerged from behind the door. My eyes nearly popped out of my face. There, strapped to the handlebars was an old birdcage, and sitting on the little swinging bird perch inside the cage was a slumped and defeated-looking Amp.

"Amp!" I screamed. "Wait!"

That was when Taylor emerged with the rest
of the bike. He looked back over his shoulder,
and his mouth dropped open in surprise. "He's

mine, Zack!" he shrieked. He pushed the big bike toward the gate and fumbled at the rope that would open the gate.

"Oh, no you don't!" I bellowed.

In one smooth movement, I leaped onto my desk and slid out of my second-story window, realizing just as my body went over my windowsill and gravity grabbed ahold of me that the ladder Olivia had leaned up against my house last night was gone.

Gone!

Using that deep part of my brain we must share with monkeys, orangutans, and chimps, my hands shot out and I managed to grab the windowsill edge.

My body's entire weight transferred to my fingertips. "Aaaaaagh!" I garbled in surprise and pain.

Behind me, I heard the gate scrape open.

There I was, dangling on the side of my house, twenty feet in the air, my feet desperately searching for a ladder that wasn't there and my fingertips begging for me to let go. All the while my brother was slipping away, kidnapping my alien roommate.

My life was so not normal.

Gasping hot breaths, I steadied myself and dared to look down. I could see the bushes far below. It looked like a mile. I heard the gate close behind me, and I grunted in desperation.

I squeezed my eyes shut. I took a deep breath. I had no choice. I let go.

07

Giving Chase

I fell like a bag of bricks.

It felt like I was falling for a full minute, but it couldn't have been more than a second or two.

My whole body tensed up before I crashed down into the bushes.

I heard a tearing sound, which I thought came from my body, but it was just my shirt. The cracking sounds, which I thought were my bones snapping on impact, were just the bush's branches splintering from my impact.

I wasn't sure how it happened, but I came to a stop upside down.

After a second I started to squirm and flop around to free myself from the shaking bush.

I could feel my ankle burning with pain, either from a sprain or a cut—I couldn't tell which. I

43

must have had scrapes everywhere because the skin on my neck, face, arms, and feet stung. My shirt ripped even more as it snagged on the splintered branches.

With a final groan, I flopped from the broken bush onto the wet grass, checking to be sure all my limbs were still attached. With an amazed glance up at my second-story window, I turned and limped off after my brother and my alien, tiny leaves and blades of grass dropping from my hair and body as I ran.

"Did someone steal your stairs?" Olivia asked with a whistle, suddenly appearing on her side of the fence.

I made a noise similar to the sound a monster would make.

"I need to talk to you," she said.

I didn't look over, and just hobbled past her toward the gate.

"Uh . . . sorry about the ladder," she said, observing me with a puzzled look as I passed her. "I should have told you I took it back."

"Gotta catch them," I said to her over my shoulder, gasping.

"Who? Your neck is bleeding a bit. And your pants are torn. I can see your boxer shorts."

I stopped at the gate and looked back at her. "I found Amp! Taylor has him!" I cried. "And he's gonna tell everyone!"

"What? How? Wait!"

I left the gate open, then limped down the driveway and out onto the street. I looked both ways. Twice. Nothing!

45

Then I saw them.

Taylor was at least ten houses away. My mom's bike wobbled unsteadily onto the street from the sidewalk. Its frame was way too big for Taylor, who wasn't very good at riding a bike in the first place.

I knew why he was on my mom's bike. He was embarrassed by his. It used to have training wheels on it, and it was painted bright orange and covered with images of a cartoon show he used to watch. He called it a "baby bike." But his inability to handle Mom's bike gave me a chance to catch him.

"Taylor, stop! You don't know what you're doing!"

I took off after them. My ankle throbbed in protest. My neck tickled. My arms and face stung. The rough street tore at the soft skin on the bottoms of my feet. In frustration, my eyes teared up. I couldn't stop it.

Down the street a car turned the corner and slowed down as it passed me, going in the opposite direction. The two adults in the car stared at me like they were witnessing a scene from a very sad

zombie movie. The man behind the wheel rolled up his window as they passed by.

With a groan of horror, I saw the face of a girl from my class in the backseat. Jade glared at me with shocked recognition, her eyes going wide as the car drove around me. I managed a pained smile and a halfhearted wave, but there was no way everyone at school wasn't going to hear about this.

But what did that matter?

An attack on Earth by an alien army would certainly drown out any gossip about a blubbering, bloody Zack McGee running down the middle of the street in his pajamas on an otherwise peaceful Saturday morning.

I stopped. It was useless. Taylor was gone.

He was meeting with people who would blow the cover off the best-kept secret in history.

"You didn't have a chance," Olivia said suddenly from somewhere behind me. She must have been running after me.

"I know." I sighed, not turning around so she couldn't see my watery eyes.

"Do you know where he was going?" she asked.

I shook my head and still didn't turn around.

She was silent for a moment. "Did you see Jade?" she asked softly. "She's nice."

"I did," I said with a sniff. I threw my arms up and let them fall back to my sides. "What a disaster," I said.

"Yup," she said. "A disaster of global proportions."

"I never thought it would end like this."

"Come back to my garage. You're bleeding. You look really weird. And I have something to tell you."

Too exhausted to argue, I turned and followed Olivia back down the street, wondering what she could possibly have to tell me that even mattered at this point.

08

First Aid

"I'd feel better if I went over and told your folks," Olivia's grandfather said, pressing a big bandage onto my neck. "Let them know you're over here and okay."

"At this point that would make things a lot worse," I said. "Trust me."

"Grandpa was a doctor in the army," Olivia said proudly.

"Not a doctor," he said, smiling at me. "A medic. But still, I've seen a lot worse."

"What's the difference between a doctor and a medic?" I asked.

"Pay grade," he mumbled, dabbing a cotton ball onto my forehead.

We were in their dusty, dim, and crowded garage. We were surrounded by boxes, crates, fishing poles, canoes, hunting gear, folded-up canvas tents, unused bikes, pots and pans, and every possible thing someone might collect over a long and adventurous lifetime.

I was sitting slumped at the end of an old lumpy couch, a frosty blue ice pack from their freezer wrapped lightly around my ankle. Olivia's grandfather had cleaned some of the bigger scrapes on my arms and face with a smelly liquid that stung more than I cared to show.

Olivia's grandfather didn't say much or ask questions as he patched me up, but Olivia had told me he wasn't a big talker.

"You'll live," he said, and patted me on my knee. Then he shuffled through the door without another word, leaving us alone in the garage.

That dusty couch was where Olivia and I had often hung out with Amp, away from the eyes of the rest of the world. I looked over at the stool Amp had usually stood on, the round seat like a little stage he used to pace around on when he'd lecture us about science and space travel and why he liked Ritz Crackers.

Knowing he'd never stand there again made the silence that now filled the garage seem almost tragic.

I shifted, trying to get comfortable. "Well, here we are. The quiet before the storm."

"I don't think Amp saw his planet—or his sun or whatever—blow up," Olivia said.

"He's wrong about almost everything," I said with sigh. "But what makes you say that?"

Olivia held up a flashlight. "Watch this. When

I turn this on, tell me if you can see the light shoot across the garage and hit the far wall."

She clicked it on. A beam of light lit up the dark and gloomy garage as a spotlight appeared on the opposite wall. She clicked it on and off a few more times, each time the light instantly appearing.

"Are we going to play shadow puppets before the end of the world?" I complained.

"No! But I'm proving a point."

"Yes, your batteries work. Point taken."

"Not that, you dimwit. I'm talking about the speed of light."

"Oh my gosh, Olivia, if this is a science lesson, my head may just melt right here and now."

"Don't be a baby. I'm talking about how long it takes light to travel from another sun to Earth."

"And why do I care? I can see that light is pretty much instant. So what? Amp is gone, and the world is about to end. Can't see why I should care."

She growled at me. "Don't you get it? I was talking to Grandpa about this. I looked it up on Google. Light travels at the same speed everywhere, about one hundred and eighty-six thousand miles per second."

"Per second? I think you mean per hour."

"No, I mean one hundred and eighty-six thousand miles per second. At that speed you could go around the Earth seven times in one second."

"I would puke for sure," I said, not getting why this was important.

"That is so fast, it's ridiculous, right?"

"Sure," I said. "Get to the point—the world as we know it is about to end."

"You're so dramatic."

"Seriously? The end of the world seems like an

appropriate time for a little drama."

"Just listen. The nearest star to our solar system is called Proxima Centauri."

"Will this be on the test?"

"Shush! Proxima Centauri is the nearest star in the whole universe of stars, okay? It's actually one of three stars in the Alpha Centauri system."

"All of this so doesn't seem important right now."

"Guess how long it would take light from that star to get here, traveling at one hundred and eighty-six thousand miles per second."

"Per second? Hmmmm. Maybe a few minutes," I guessed with a shrug.

"No, it would take 4.37 light-years."

"Light-years?"

"Yes, a light-year is the distance light can travel in one year."

"That sounds far. But how far is that in miles?"

Olivia looked up and thought. "I didn't figure it out exactly . . . but it's about twenty-five trillion miles away from here."

I stared at her for a moment. "Just thinking about that hurts my face."

"All of this means that the light flash or what-ever Amp saw happened years ago. It didn't happen just now. It would take forever for that light to reach us here on Earth."

"So?"

"Don't you get it?" Olivia asked. "I think the light he saw might be . . . It might mean the invasion of Earth is about to start."

"I know! What do you think I've been saying all this time? I don't need trillions of miles to know that. The attack alarm on his spaceship is going off!"

"It is? Oh my gosh, Zack, why didn't you say that in the first place, you bubble brain?"

"The Erdian invasion is about to begin," I said, still not believing what I knew to be true.

"Oh my gosh! We have to tell Amp!" Olivia shrieked, jumping up.

"Why do you think I fell out of my window and ran down the street like human roadkill?"

The gravity of the situation seemed to sweep over her face. She slapped her cheeks and kept her hands there. "And your brother is . . ."

"Yup," I said.

We both heard the screen door of Olivia's house open with a sudden bang. "Olivia, hurry, you two should come see what's on TV!" Olivia's grandfather shouted from the front door.

Olivia and I exchanged a glance.

"It's started," she whispered.

09

Live with Taylor McGee

"Well, Ted," a female TV reporter said into her microphone, "as you can see from all the commotion behind me, a young second-grader from Reed School named Taylor McGee has announced that he has found an alien. It's caused a lot of excitement here on the steps of the main library."

I couldn't believe what I was seeing. The reporter didn't seem upset or worried; she seemed to think the whole thing was funny, like a prank or a big joke. She wasn't getting it. This was the biggest news story in the history of the world.

A man's voice asked the reporter a question. "Hold on, Ann, do you mean, like, little green men from Mars?"

The reporter laughed. "Exactly, Ted—except

this alien reportedly is blue."

"Did the alien ask to be taken to our leader?"

"I'm not sure," the reporter said, laughing. She looked behind her at a confused crowd of reporters, police officers, firefighters, and ordinary curious citizens holding up their camera phones. "It's pretty tiny for an alien."

"How does she know how big an alien is supposed to be?" I croaked.

"Ann, so what did the alien look like?"

"It's hard to describe, Ted. Imagine a squirrel that's been shaved and painted blue."

"A squirrel?" Olivia burst out angrily from behind me.

"Please, you two, sit down," Olivia's grandpa said from the couch. "I can't see the screen."

The reporter looked down at her notepad. "Ted, some of the other reporters here said it also looks like . . . a large blue frog. One told me it looked like moldy bread dough. Another described it as a baby rabbit, or a naked mole rat with a skin condition."

"A naked mole rat with a skin condition?" Olivia roared.

"Moldy blue bread dough?" I snapped. "That's idiotic!"

I was trying to spot my brother in the churning swarm of the crowd behind the reporter. The scene was chaotic. I recognized the front of the library, which was just a few streets down from my house. I could be there in just minutes, but I couldn't pull myself away from the out-of-control scene taking place before my eyes.

"The young man seemed convinced that he has an alien in his cage," the woman said directly into the camera. She shook her head. "And I'll admit, Ted, the creature was moving, and I honestly can't say exactly what I saw."

That was when I saw a man lift Taylor above the crowd and onto his shoulders. Taylor was still holding the birdcage, his arms wrapped tightly around it. Hands pulled and poked at the cage. For a split second I could see Amp's tiny body being tossed around inside the cage.

"There he is!" Olivia shouted, falling to her knees next to me and jabbing her finger at the screen. "I can see Amp!"

61

"Who's Amp?" Olivia's grandfather asked. "I can't see anything!"

When the man turned, I could see it was Mr. Prentiss. I could tell from the look on his face he was worried for Taylor's safety—even his own safety! The camera was jostled, and the video cut out for a second. An intense panic seemed to be sweeping over the crowd.

"No!" I shouted, pressing both of my hands onto the TV screen. I was just six inches from the screen now. "Get out of there, Taylor!" I shouted at the screen.

"What's happening?" Olivia's grandfather asked. "Is that your brother in the middle of that mess?"

"Go, go, go!" Olivia hollered at the TV screen.

The crowd seemed to chase Taylor and his cage. Hands pulled at the cage and tugged on Taylor's shirt. Mr. Prentiss pushed through the crowd. I could see Taylor was crying. I could no longer see Amp.

"You can see, Ted, that things are getting out of hand down here. The police are pushing into the crowd. They are . . . Several people have . . . Authorities are trying to restore order."

"It's turning into a riot," Olivia whispered.

I lost Taylor and Mr. Prentiss in the crowd. The cameraman appeared to be running after Taylor and Mr. Prentiss, but he stumbled to the ground. Running bodies passed in front of the camera. An older woman was knocked down.

I glimpsed Taylor and Mr. Prentiss being pushed

into a large black car with tinted windows. The man who opened the door wore sunglasses and looked as large as a barn.

"They're getting into that car!" Olivia said, jabbing her finger onto the screen.

"Where are they taking him?" I asked.

The car pulled quickly away, being led by four police motorcycles with their red-and-blue lights blinking. Some people even ran after the car as it pulled away from the curb and made its way slowly through the growing crowd out in front of the library.

"I'm not sure what's going on, Ted," the reporter said from somewhere offscreen. "I've never been . . . The crowd seemed to panic. It's like electricity is in the air. I'm not sure what that boy has, but the crowd here—"

The screen turned black.

I spun around, and Olivia's grandfather was holding the remote control. He had turned off the TV. "You two need to tell me what's going on."

"Grandpa, you better sit down," Olivia whispered in the sudden silence.

"I am sitting," he said simply.

"Oh, right," Olivia said, then looked uncomfortably at me.

I swallowed. "We've been keeping a secret," I said while looking at Olivia, then pivoted my head toward Olivia's grandfather. "That really is an alien in the birdcage."

"Nonsense," he said quietly.

I nodded. "He's been living in my room. He's from the planet Erde. He likes to eat Ritz Crackers, SweeTarts, and sometimes sunflowers seeds. And I'm going to go get his spaceship to prove it to you."

Busted

Things seemed foggy.

I really should have eaten breakfast.

It felt like I was underwater. I pushed through the air, which seemed thicker than usual. From Olivia's backyard, I saw a giant white van screech to a stop out in front of our house. Three men in white jumpsuits rushed out from behind the doors and ran to the back of the van. Written on the side of the van in big black letters were the words HAZARDOUS MATERIAL CONTAINMENT RESPONSE TEAM. A bar of lights on the top of the van blinked a bright yellow. Two police officers on motorcycles pulled up beside the van a moment later.

Olivia and I ducked down and snuck her grandpa's ladder around the back and leaned it against my house. If we were going to sneak Amp's spaceship out of my house, we were going to have to be quick about it.

I climbed that ladder like a ninja after seven cups of coffee. I went through my window so fast that I spilled across my desk and kicked over my lamp, which proceeded to fall onto the back of my head after I face-planted into the carpet. The metal lampshade then made a loud *ting* after it bounced off the back of my skull and landed on the ground.

"Smooth move," Olivia said from above me, her head still in the window. "I bet if you tried, you could make more noise."

I replaced the lamp and rubbed the painful lump now rising on the back of my head. I rushed into the bathroom and pulled yesterday's dirty clothes out of the hamper. When I came out, Olivia had scrambled over the desk and was in the closet looking for Amp's spaceship—the *Dingle*.

"Zack, come quick," Olivia said from the closet. "We have a problem."

"What now?" I followed her into the closet and saw what she was looking at.

The wool blanket that covered Amp's space-ship was in a heap, and the spaceship was gone. I picked up the blanket, as if I half expected the *Dingle* to drop out. It didn't. It was gone.

"It— It— It was right here," I stammered. "I just saw it before I ran after Amp. This makes no sense."

Olivia shook her head. "None of this makes sense."

11

Floater

"It's gone!" I cried. "The *Dingle* is gone."

"Now my grandpa will never believe us," Olivia said.

"Forget about your grandpa," I said, still clutching the wool blanket. "Now Amp will never be able to get back home!" Loud voices echoed from downstairs. Another blaring siren came roaring up my street.

I shook the blanket one last time then dropped it. "They're going to put me in jail for secretly keeping an alien in my house. I can't go to jail. I haven't even finished fourth grade!"

I stared at the dark corner of my closet, where the *Dingle* had rested peacefully for the last few months. This was all my fault. I tried to hold it back, but I couldn't. I started to cry. Hot tears came rolling down my cheeks like water over the rim of a clogged toilet.

Olivia patted my shoulder from behind, but I didn't turn around.

"Thanks," I said with a tight croaky voice. "You're a good friend."

"No, you ninny, look," she said.

I peeked over my shoulder to see that she was pointing up. I followed her eyes to the ceiling of my closet, and there floated Amp's spaceship, silently bobbing in the corner.

"How is it flying?" I said with a sniff.

"No idea," Olivia whispered.

We stared at it in silence. It had gotten tangled up in some string. It looked like a golden balloon pulling on a leash.

I wiped the tears from my cheeks with the back of my hand. Olivia jumped up, but she couldn't untangle the string.

"Anybody up there?" a strange man's voice called from the bottom of the stairs. "My name is Agent Musson, and I have a warrant to search this house."

Olivia and I made bug eyes at each other. Neither of us made a peep. I heard him open the door to Taylor's room. He must have stepped on some part of one of Taylor's unfinished experiments, because he gave a yelp when it made a strange noise. Without speaking, I quickly tiptoed out of the closet, grabbed my desk chair, and carried it into the closet. I put my hand on Olivia's head for balance, climbed on top of the chair, and with a yank I pulled the spaceship free from the drooping string.

"Eww . . . his ship is warm," I whispered when I got the spaceship under my arm.

"Hurry, I hear more footsteps," Olivia hissed.

At that moment we shut the closet door just as my bedroom door swung open. I was still on the chair, the palm of my hand still pressed on the top of Olivia's head. We both stood as still as we could, trying not to breath.

"Is anyone in here?" the man asked. "This is the FBI, and this area is under investigation."

Olivia and I stared at each other, straining not to move or make a noise. I held my breath. I could hear footsteps walk into my room, pause for a few seconds, then exit. The floor creaked out in the hall, which meant the agent was heading back to Taylor's room.

"Older brother's room is a mess, but it looks clear!" the man's voice boomed, apparently to someone downstairs.

Olivia tapped my arm and pointed to the side of the *Dingle*. Next to the flashing purple invasion warning light I had seen earlier was what appeared to be the shape of an Erdian, like Amp's perfect silhouette, also flashing in purple.

I shrugged. I stepped down from the chair and listened for the agent. Olivia poked her head out

73

of the closet. "The coast is clear," she whispered. "For now."

"Look," I said. After untangling the spaceship from the string, I'd noticed it weighed nothing.

It was like holding a party balloon filled with warm helium. Normally, Amp's spaceship was pretty heavy. I pulled my palms away from the sides of the ship, and it floated in the air for a second, and then, like a tiny blimp, headed for the open window. I stepped forward and grabbed it again. It floated patiently in my hands, but I could tell it wanted to float away.

"I've got it!" I whispered. "It's like a homing device. It's trying to go to Amp. To rescue him or something. Like in those old Westerns, the cowboy movies, when the good guy's horse returns to help him escape and catch him in the saddle when he jumps out of a second-story window."

Olivia blinked at Zack. "I don't watch those kinds of movies."

I could hear the agents moving around in Taylor's room, switching his many homemade robots on and off. "Lots of tech in here. We should also toss the older brother's room—just to be on the safe side."

As quickly and quietly as she could, Olivia crawled across my desk and out the window, her eyes on the open door the whole time. "C'mon," she whispered.

I grabbed my scissors out of the jar on my desk and ran back into the closet and snipped off a length of the string. I tied it quickly around the spaceship's middle.

I followed Olivia out the window. "Check it out—I've got a balloon," I told her as we backed down the ladder.

"Quit messing around," she growled. "I think they're coming into the backyard."

The spaceship pulled at the string, but it wasn't too hard to hold on to as I climbed out over my desk and onto the ladder. The *Dingle* strained against the string and floated behind me.

Another man in a suit came through the back-yard gate, walking backward and unrolling plastic yellow crime scene tape. Holding our breaths, we made it through the fence and into Olivia's back-yard before he ever turned around.

We were back in business.

I was already pretty confident I had a plan to rescue Amp from whatever prison now held him.

12

Shock and Awe

"It's a miracle," Olivia's grandfather said, rubbing his hands gently down both sides of Amp's spaceship.

The three of us were standing in their kitchen. I looked at Olivia, but she only shrugged.

Olivia's grandfather gently poked the floating ship with his index finger and studied it carefully. "This material. It's warm. And it glows. There are no seams. It's light but strong. I never would have believed it."

"Yes, we figured you'd believe us once you saw this," Olivia said.

"Pretty cool, huh?" I said. "We never knew it could float like this. It just started. Usually, it's kinda heavy."

He shook his head in wonder. "It hovers like it

weighs nothing. What is the power source? What is the mechanism that keeps it afloat?"

"We . . . we don't know too much about it, actually," I said. "It can't blast off. It got damaged when it crash-landed. I know its name: the *Dingle*."

"The *Dingle*? What a terrible name for such a magnificent machine."

"Grandpa, we think it's trying to get back to Amp," Olivia said. "It's going to lead us to him. We're going to rescue Amp."

"Who is Amp again?" he said, sinking slowly into a kitchen chair.

"The tiny alien we've been telling you about," Olivia said. "The one who drove this through space and time to get here. He's been living in Zack's bedroom. Sorry to keep such a secret from you, but we decided it was the best for everyone."

"This is why you were interested in the tele-scope?" he mumbled, remembering.

I nodded. "And now that everybody already knows, we can tell you."

"Oh, thanks," he said in a faraway voice.

He seemed a bit overwhelmed by everything. Who could blame him? It was a lot to take in all at once. He took his glasses off and cleaned them with a bit of fuzzy cloth he pulled from his pocket. He returned the glasses to their usual spot and blinked at the metallic spaceship that pulled on its string and hovered just above his kitchen table.

Olivia fidgeted. "Grandpa, things are kind of urgent at the moment."

He cleared his throat and fixed his eyes on me for the first time since we'd walked in with the *Dingle* on a string. "And how do you propose to use this to track down your friend?"

"We'll hold the string out of the truck window," Olivia explained. "That's how we'll know when to turn and stuff. We'll just follow the *Dingle*."

He looked at us both. "This is crazy, you two."

"I know," Olivia said, putting a hand on her grandfather's shoulder. "But the FBI is searching Zack's house right now, and they'll probably be at our door in a few minutes. They'll put two and two together."

He chuckled and shook his head in disbelief. "How did I end up in a kitchen with Bonnie and Clyde?" he said.

"Who?" Olivia asked.

"It's a movie," I said, and sighed. "About bank robbers from the old days. My parents won't let me watch it."

"Let me get my keys," he said, and shuffled out of the kitchen in his slippers.

Olivia and I smiled at each other. Our plan was set. Things were starting to look up. And then: the power went out. In a breath the neighborhood outside seemed to go silent all around us.

Olivia went to the window. "What's that mean? Is the FBI cutting off the power? Standard procedure probably."

"No, it's not the FBI. It's the . . . the invasion," I whispered. "It's starting. I just know it."

Olivia gasped and turned from the window. "You can't be sure."

I looked at the two lights blinking on the side of Amp's ship, the one with Amp's shape and the other warning of the invasion.

"I'm sure."

Olivia blew out a big breath. "We need to get Amp more than ever. And soon. He's the only one who can prevent the attack."

Olivia's grandfather stepped into the kitchen. He now wore sunglasses, a fishing vest with about forty pockets, some rugged boots, and a flimsy hat with a brim that went all the way around for sun protection. "Let's do this," he said simply.

He stepped over to me and tied the end of the string I was holding to a thick piece of wood that had had a hole drilled through the middle of it. He

81

tied a knot that looked complicated yet simple, one like a true fisherman would have tied.

The stick was about a foot long and looked like it may have at one time been part of a broom handle. "What's that for?" I asked.

"You don't want to lose ahold of that thing," he said, nodding to the *Dingle*. "Once you've got a live one on the line, you don't want it slipping off. And besides, that spaceship is our golden ticket."

"Grandpa, there's one more thing."

"What? Let me guess: you want to drive?" he said, with a smirk.

"No," Olivia said uncomfortably. "We think the power went out because our friend's planet is about to attack this one. Like millions of tiny Erdians . . . They're going to invade Earth. They can't hurt us—not really. Their weapons are actually just kind of ticklish. But we're worried about them. They're complete pains to have as roommates, but we don't want to see millions of them get squished, either. Amp is the only one who can stop them. We need to break him free."

Olivia's grandfather looked at both of us. He

83

nodded slowly, processing this new information. "I don't know what to think of any of this. The rules are kind of out the window. So we'd better get started and make it up as we go, then, hadn't we?"

And with that, we set off to save the world in a muddy creaky truck that was following a driverless spaceship tied to a string.

13

Camp Sutter

By the time we pulled to the side of the road, it was late at night and we were all exhausted.

We had parked just off a dark road far outside of town. We now sat in silence, the engine clicking in the darkness.

If you thought it'd be easy to follow a spaceship at the end of a string, you'd have been mistaken. Sometimes you turn left when it's just the breeze blowing your spaceship. Sometimes you make a U-turn only to take another U-turn in about thirty feet.

We'd expected to reach our destination in minutes, but we wound up driving around for hours.

Traffic signals weren't working because of the power outage, so traffic was terrible. We had to stop for gas twice. We went through a drive-thru for burgers, fries, and shakes, and ate in the car.

Olivia's grandpa had a cell phone, but it wasn't working for some reason. So at one gas station I had asked to use the phone, and I'd left my parents a message on our house's answering machine.

I told them I had gone fishing with Olivia's grandpa and would be back late. This was not technically a lie—I was trying to catch an Erdian—but it certainly was not the whole story.

Now the three of us got out and stretched our muscles next to the truck under some towering pine trees. My neck was stiff from leaning out of the window and looking up at the balloon.

Farther up the road was Camp Sutter, which Olivia's grandpa told us was a large National Guard base. Parked in front of the camp were six or seven news vans with big broadcasting antennas extending from their roofs. Bright lights illuminated reporters, each holding a microphone and gesturing to the tall wire fence behind them. We watched as guards stood in front of the gates and spoke to each person who wanted to get in. A few had large dogs on leashes.

"How are we supposed to get in there?" Olivia asked.

We watched several thunderous helicopters land on the far side of a big building, and we could see a few dozen people entering and exiting.

"That has to be where Amp is," I said, pointing, quickly putting my hand back on the stick I was holding because the spaceship was really straining to go toward the camp.

"Notice they have big lights set up," Olivia observed. "The power is out here, too."

Six cars drove quickly by us on the road. We stood on the other side of the truck, so I don't think they even knew we were there. In the first car I saw four men in suits who looked pretty tense. Then, in the third car, I saw my parents and Aunt Joni, all looking worried and sick.

"That's my mom, dad, and aunt," I said.

"I saw them," Olivia said. "Taylor must be here, too."

Mr. Prentiss was in the last car, talking on his phone. Luckily, it was inky dark on the road, and the headlights left us and Amp's spaceship hidden in the shadows.

"Look at the stars," Olivia's grandpa whispered.

"Whoa. There're billions," Olivia said.

"There are too many," Olivia's grandpa said in a strange voice. "And they're making a noise."

It was true. A strange, distant, high-pitched humming sound filled the air. I would have thought it was a mosquito flying by my ear, but it was steady and unchanging.

I gulped. "You don't think that's—" The words got caught in my throat.

"The Erdians?" Olivia said next to me. "Is that them? You can hardly see them. And why aren't they doing anything?"

Olivia's grandpa shuffled his feet nervously. "They must have a cloaking technology of some kind so nobody can see them on radar. Kids, we need to report this."

And that was when my feet left the ground.

14

Lift-off

"**Z**ack!" Olivia screamed.

I was flying.

Or balloon skiing.

Or sky surfing.

"Aaaaaagh!" I yelped as the balloon pulled the kite string as tight as a wire. I kept rising in the air and drifting over the road.

"Let go, Zack!" Olivia's grandfather shouted. "Let it go!"

I almost listened to his command, but then I looked down. I was already ten feet in the air.

Olivia ran at me through the dark—she was good in emergencies! She jumped up, but it was no use. I could see Olivia's dark figure sprawled out in the middle of the road. I was easily twenty feet in the air. I had already fallen from this height earlier

today, and I was not going to repeat that mistake!

I was rising incredibly fast. The world spun under me.

I cleared the top of the towering trees. My heart was thundering, and my breath was ragged with fear. I hadn't tied my shoes, so they fell off. I could feel the moist air seeping in through my socks.

I was soon flying high over the bright lights of the reporters outside the gate.

I had no idea how high I was, but I knew if I let go now—or if the string broke—I'd become road pizza, a puddle of the kid formerly known as Zack McGee.

The thought of being pulled up into the sky with the creepy army of hovering Erdian ships crossed my mind. But it soon became clear that the *Dingle* was on a rescue mission. We were heading toward the roof of the big building with all the activity going on around it.

I was getting dizzy from so much spinning. I searched the dark sky as best I could for approaching helicopters, which would surely be bad news for me.

Then the spaceship started to sink. I could hear voices and the sounds of vehicles below. I could see the headlights of the cars that had passed us on the road now pulling up near the big building.

It was hard to be sure because I was now spinning so fast at the end of the string, I was afraid it would snap.

In the next moment I was touching down in just my socks on the smooth roof of the biggest building.

I had not been that dizzy since I got spun around for my turn at Pin the Tail on the Donkey at Nino Sasso's birthday party in the first grade.

I stumbled about for a full minute, yanking the *Dingle* after me. I was finally able to get my footing. I waited for my brain to stop spinning inside my skull.

The *Dingle* landed gently next to a large open tube that extended a foot through the roof. Light from inside the building beamed out. The tube had a screen on top of it that I lifted off easily. It was big enough to look into, but I couldn't have fit my body inside even if I'd wanted to.

93

I looked down and couldn't believe my eyes. Amp was in a large plastic tub twenty feet below me. It was resting on a large white table. Two men in white lab coats where taking photos of him with a digital camera that flashed over and over.

Amp was pacing back and forth. He looked agitated. He was posing in silly ways. Sticking out his tongue rudely. Shaking his butt at the camera. Making faces.

I tried to fit the spaceship through the tube, but the ship was too wide.

I put my face against the tube's opening, closed my eyes, and concentrated. "Amp!?" I mind-shouted.

I could see his body flinch. I also noticed that the two guys in lab coats had left him.

"Zack?" I heard him say quietly in his mind. "Are you here with your parents? I can hear them."

"No!" I snapped at him with my mind. "I'm on the roof above you." I watched him look up slowly.

"What? Oh, now I see you," he said excitedly. "You look ridiculous."

"Better than you do."

"Where have you been? Get me out of this floofy place!"

I made a face. "Oh? What about giving up? I thought it was all over. I thought you didn't care anymore."

I could tell he didn't like that because he hopped around in frustration. "Forget about that! I was wrong. I can see that now. The invasion is about to begin!" his voice echoed inside my skull. "They've got two dozen scientists gathered outside this room. They're talking about starting the

95

probe. I thought aliens probed humans—I didn't realize it went the other way around. Get me out of here right now!"

"Your spaceship almost killed me getting here!"

"It's here? You have the *Dingle*?"

"Yes. It flew me up here. It almost turned me into road pizza!"

"What is road pizza?"

"Never mind. Can you get up here?"

"I can't even get out of this bowl!" he exclaimed, kicking the plastic tub that held him. "I can't fly, you know!"

"And what? You think I'm Peter Pan?"

"The peanut butter?"

"Ugh! I can't just walk in there and ask to see their lost and found box!"

I was getting frustrated. I pulled my face out of the tube and grabbed my head. "Think, think, think," I whispered.

I looked around me in the dark, but besides a few antennas, an old soda can, and a rusty wire clothes hanger, there was nothing up there to help me.

That was when I got either the best idea of my life—or the worst. And there was only one way to find out which.

Escape

Standing on the roof in my underwear was a lot colder than I'd expected.

My body started shivering as I lowered my tied-together clothes through the hole.

I started with the string I untied from the *Dingle*. I tied it to the end of my belt, and I lowered the two into the pipe.

But when I lowered it through the pipe, it only got about halfway down to Amp.

"Do you think I'm a giraffe?" Amp shouted in my head. "Or a kangaroo? I can't reach that!"

"Oh, be quiet," I growled, pulling the string and my belt back up through the opening.

So I pulled off my socks and tied them together, and then I yanked off my shirt and pants and tied the end of one sock to a pant leg and the other end to a shirt sleeve. Then I tied the other sleeve to the string.

And eventually I was standing in the dark in my boxers. I dropped the crazy rope of string, belt, pants, and socks back down through the open pipe. The tub that held Amp was positioned right under the open-air vent, so all he'd need to do was hop on and get pulled up.

"I still can't quite reach it," he said, gasping in my head. "How tall do you think I am?"

"I don't think you're tall at all," I bellowed inside my mind. "But I thought you could at least jump a little."

"They're outside the door," he mind-whispered. "At least you tried, Zack."

"Get out of my head and let me think," I said. I looked around in the dark in desperation. I had one last idea.

Using my bare foot, I reached out and pulled the clothes hanger to me, never letting go of the stretched-out sock in my fist. I quickly smooshed the hanger flat against my bare ribs—the hanger was freezing—and jammed its hook though my shirt sleeve. I dropped the hanger and my whole arm through the hole.

"Ouch!" Amp screeched in my head. "You hit me on the head with your belt buckle."

"No one has ever complained so much during a rescue! Are you holding on? I can't see; my arm is jammed into this pipe."

That was when I heard shouting down below. Chairs being knocked over and glass breaking. I heard a scream. Then someone shouted, "The beast is escaping!"

The beast? Amp is a lot of things, but he's hardly a beast.

I started pulling up fast, one hand over the other. First the hanger, then the socks, then the pants, then the string, then belt buckle. With an annoyed look on his face, Amp emerged from the pipe holding the belt buckle.

"It's about time," he said, rolling his eyes.

The air filled with a shrill, earsplitting alarm. Voices shouted from below. Someone barked commands outside. Somebody was climbing up the metal ladder that was attached to the side of the building and that ended at the roof's edge.

"We're trapped," I said.

"Is that how you dress for a daring rescue?" Amp snickered, hopping over to his spaceship. He placed his little three-fingered hand on his blinking silhouette, and a tiny hatch opened with a click.

An angry soldier's face appeared in the dark at the top of the ladder, just feet away. "Don't move!" he shouted, pointing at me. "You are under arrest!"

"Seriously?" I squeaked. The door on the *Dingle* closed again with a little snick noise.

"There's a kid in his underwear up here!" the soldier hollered back down the ladder. "The beast has him!"

The soldier sprung from the ladder and landed on his big black boots in front of me. He got into a fighting position, like he was ready to do battle.

"Take it easy, sir," I quivered. "I give up!" I raised my hands in surrender.

"Go, Amp, go!" I commanded with my mind. "Now's your chance!"

"Hold on," Amp said inside my head.

"Hold on to what?" I said aloud.

The soldier looked at me. "Hold on to what?" he asked. "What does that—"

Just then the *Dingle* shot up with a whoosh and punched me in the gut.

Acting on reflexes alone, my arms wrapped around the spaceship like I had just caught a forty-mile-an-hour football pass.

Then I was flying, spinning like a human helicopter over the roof.

The soldier was chasing us, his hands outstretched at me.

My boxers flapped in the wind.

"Boy, you're heavy!" Amp said in my head.

"Stop! That's a direct order! You get back here!" the soldier yelled.

The soldier ran out of roof and stopped at the edge, his arms flailing as he worked to keep his balance.

Now I was high in the air again for the second time that night. The camp below me had exploded with activity. Soldiers, men in suits, people in lab coats, and others I couldn't make out spilled from the building and searched the dark sky for us.

I didn't think flying could be any more uncomfortable than hanging on to a stick at the end of string, but this topped it.

I was practically naked, spinning like a top, and wobbling back and forth over a floating ball that rose and dove through the air.

"Problems with the stabilizers," Amp growled in my head.

"Olivia and her grandpa!" I said as best I could with my brain. "They're on the road. Outside the main gate. Three hundred yards or so."

"Got it," Amp replied sharply, sounding more like himself. "Just hold on."

"I assume going back for my clothes is out of the question?" I said jokingly.

"Yes, much too risky," Amp replied. "Especially since it seems the invasion has begun."

And as we rose into the air, thousands of Erdian spaceships descended all around us.

My life was not dull.

But there was still much left to be done.

I'd managed to save Amp. Now I had to save Earth.

...TO BE CONTINUED

Try It Yourself: Hover-Ship

When Zack and Olivia sneak back into Zack's room to rescue the *Dingle*, they discover a shocking surprise: Amp's ship is hovering in midair, all by itself! How on Earth would such a thing be possible? Even though we've dreamed of hovering cars and flying skateboards for ages, you sadly still don't see any real-life versions around town.

But it turns out that even though you can't ride a hover-bike to school (yet), there are real-life ways to make objects hover in midair in just the same way the *Dingle* can—using science!

Invisible Forces

Imagine holding a toy airplane in your hand and zooming it around the house. Though it's not flying by itself, the airplane is still positioned in midair. It's just that your hand is holding it there. You already know why you have to hold it there with your hand: you have to counter the force of gravity on the airplane. If you let go, the airplane will drop to the ground—pulled downward by gravity.

What about a paper airplane? You can make it fly through the air by itself with a throw. Why doesn't it fall right to the ground without you holding it up? In this case, your hand isn't countering the force of gravity—the air in the house is. Even though you can't see it, the air is doing just the same job your hand was. It's applying an upward force to the airplane that's equal to the force of gravity pulling down.

For anything to hover above the ground— anything at all—an invisible game of tug-of-war is being played. *Something* is exerting a force on the hovering object that's exactly the same strength as the force of gravity pulling it down.

Thing	Type of Force that Fights Gravity
Airplane	Air pressure difference across wings
Helicopter or drone (like a quadcopter)	Acceleration force from pushing air downward
Maglev bullet train	Electromagnetic force
Hot-air balloon	Buoyancy in air
Hair standing up on end from static electricity	Electrostatic repulsion
"Magic Wand" toy	Electrostatic repulsion
Amp's ship, the *Dingle*	Electromagnetic force

Most of the hovering and flying forces listed are impractical for indoor use. Airplanes have to fly super-fast, helicopters and drones have to spin their blades at high speed, hot-air balloons are huge, and electrostatic forces are not very strong.

To get something smaller to hover in a more practical way, we might choose to look to another force to counter the downward force of gravity. Electromagnetic forces are a great option because they're pretty easy to create or find and control. And as you might remember from *Alien in My Pocket: The Science UnFair*, Amp brought special alien technology to Earth that can control Earth's magnetic field, which makes it possible to exert *huge* forces on any objects that can also interact with magnetic fields. This is how the *Dingle* can float in midair without propellers: it bends the Earth's magnetic field around to exert forces on itself which counter gravity's downward pull.

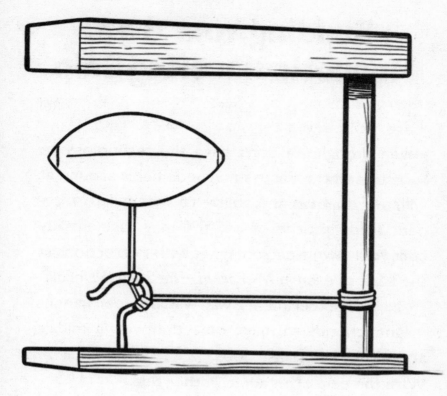

Building Your Own Magnetic Hovering Ship

Even though we don't have the technology to just bend the Earth's magnetic fields around at will, we do have the ability to manipulate magnetic fields in other ways. You may have already built your own electromagnet with instructions in the back of *Alien in My Pocket: The Science UnFair.*

In this experiment, we will use permanent magnetic fields to make objects hover in midair almost like the *Dingle* does.

With the help of an adult, gather these materials:

Materials for the dock:

- A small block of wood, like a 1x4, that's about 6 inches long, for the base
- Another small piece of wood for the top, about 5 inches long, and a bit more narrow than the 1x4 base
- A dowel rod ½ inch in diameter, about 7 inches long
- A threaded hook, like you might hang a picture with

- Two strong cylindrical magnets—one should be solid and about ½ inch in diameter (like **D88-N52** from K&J Magnetics—www.kjmagnetics.com) and the other should have a hole in it (like **R828** from K&J Magnetics)
- About a foot of string, in a size that fits through the second magnet's hole
- Wood glue

Materials for the ship:
- Paper—ideally nice and thick, like construction paper
- Colored pencils or pens for decorating
- Scotch tape

Tools:
- A drill
- A drill bit the same diameter as the dowel rod and the magnet without the hole (½ inch)
- A drill bit slightly smaller than the threads on the threaded hook
- Scissors
- Safety glasses
- Measuring tape

Step 1: Drill all the holes

1. Safety first: Put on your safety glasses
2. Use the ½-inch drill bit to drill a hole about ¾ inch away from one end of both the base and the top beam
3. Use the ½-inch drill bit to drill a hole about 4 ¼ inches away from the same end of top beam
4. Use the tiny drill bit to drill a hole in the base about 4 ¼ inches away from the same end of the base

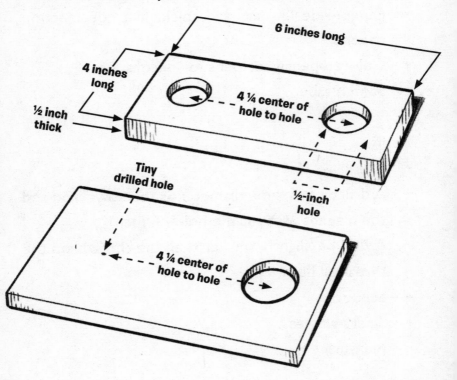

6 inches long

4 inches long

½ inch thick

4 ¼ center of hole to hole

½-inch hole

Tiny drilled hole

4 ¼ center of hole to hole

Step 2: Install the top magnet

Add a small amount of glue to the ½-inch hole in the top beam. Press the solid cylinder magnet into the hole. You might use the base block of wood to push against the magnet so you can apply more force. Push it all the way in as shown below.

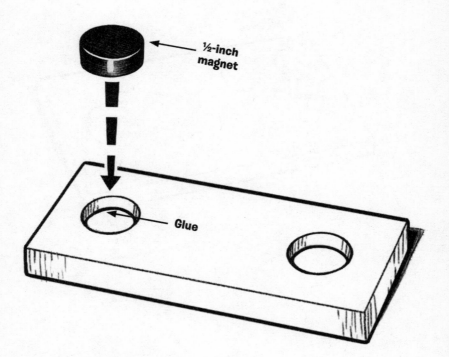

½-inch magnet

Glue

Step 3: Install the hook

Screw the hook into the small hole in the base. Be careful not to overtighten it!

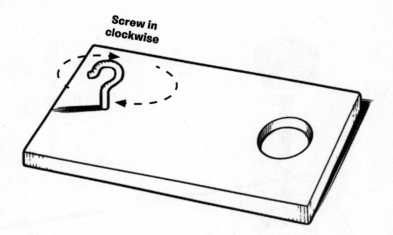

Screw in clockwise

Step 4: Join the top beam to the base using the dowel rod

Put a small dab of glue in the ½-inch diameter holes in both the base and the top beam. Install the dowel rod into the top beam, giving it a twist as you push it in. Then install the bottom of the dowel (with top beam attached) into the base with a twist as you push it in. Twist the top beam so it's parallel to the base.

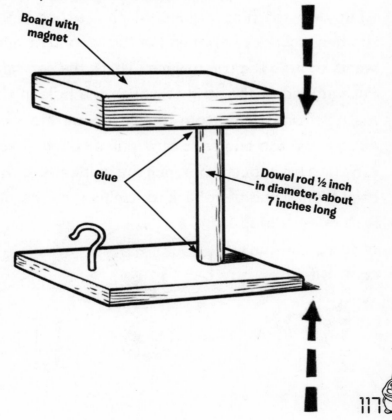

Board with magnet

Glue

Dowel rod ½ inch in diameter, about 7 inches long

Step 5: Wait a while for the glue to dry

This is the hardest part! It usually will take a few hours at least. If your dowel rod had a really tight fit, you might not need to wait as long to proceed.

Step 6: Tie the second magnet to the string

Put the second magnet (the one with the hole in it) up near the first magnet, which is sitting in the top beam. Check which end of the second magnet wants to grab the top magnet. That's the top side. Push an end of the string through the hole in the magnet from the bottom to the top and tie a big knot in the top end so it can't pull through. If you can't tie a big enough knot, pull the string all the way back around and tie it back to itself so the magnet is stuck on a loop of string and can't come off.

2nd ½-inch magnet with a hole

Step 7: Attach the magnet's string to the structure

Allow the magnet tied with the string to grab the magnet glued to the top beam, so the string is hanging down. Wrap the string around the hook, and then tie it to the dowel rod. Try using a clove hitch—it's the best way to tie a rope or string to something solid and round. Add some tape to help hold the string in place on the dowel.

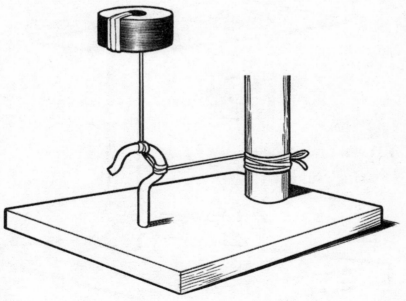

Step 8: Make it hover

Wrap the string many times around the hook until the bottom magnet can't touch the top magnet anymore. Now bring the magnet back up to the top near the stationary magnet—can it stay up all by itself? If so, great! It's hovering!

If the magnet can't stay up all by itself, unwind a couple of wraps of string.

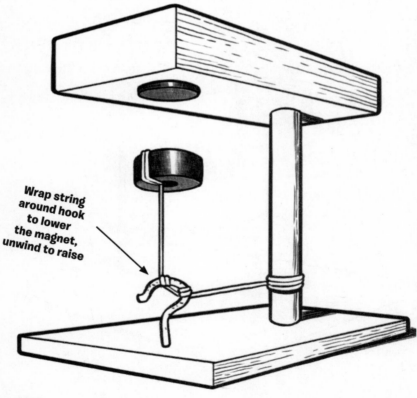

Wrap string around hook to lower the magnet, unwind to raise

Step 9: Getting it dialed

To make the science sculpture look as cool as possible, it's fun to have as much space as you can between the top magnet and the bottom magnet. Once the magnet underneath is hovering in the air, held in place by the string, shorten the string by adding one wrap at a time to the hook. With each wrap, the gap between the magnets grows. Try to adjust it so the magnet is barely held in place. Voilà! A magnet, hovering in space! You may notice that the farther away from the top beam your magnet hovers, the more slowly it moves, and the more it appears to be floating all by itself in space.

121

Step 10: Add the ship!

Now that you've got a magnet that can hover, it's time to put a spaceship on it. Do your best to copy the pattern for Amp's ship, the *Dingle,* onto your own piece of construction paper. Color it in if you want. Then cut it out, fold the tabs in, bend the paper at the dotted lines, and create the shape of Amp's tiny spacecraft. There should be a hole in the bottom big enough to pass the magnet through. Flip the whole structure upside down so the magnet is hanging downward with gravity—then drop the magnet through the hole in the ship, carefully hold it in place, and turn the whole assembly back upright. Look, it's the *Dingle* hovering in midair, ready to go rescue Amp!

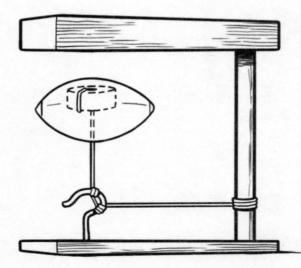

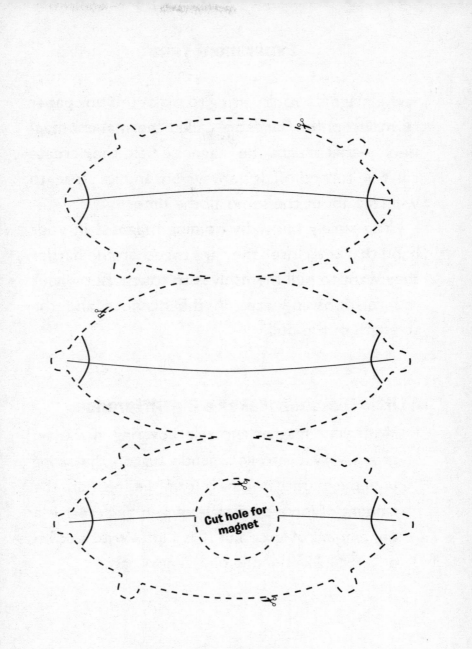

Cut hole for magnet

Experiment Time

The magnets you're using to make the tiny paper model of the *Dingle* are called "permanent magnets"—that means the magnetic field they create can't be turned off. It's always on, and its strength will stay about the same all the time.

You surely know by holding magnets in your hand that the closer they are together, the harder they want to pull themselves to touch. But what's the relationship between the distance and the strength of the pull?

A Little Distance Makes a Big Difference

1. With your magnet and ship hovering in the air, give a very controlled, gentle tug on the string until the magnet falls away from the top. Rate the amount of force on a scale of 1–10, where 1 is a tiny amount of force and 10 is a lot. Write it down on a table like the one on the next page:

Number of Wraps Undone	Amount of Force (your rating on a scale of 1–10)
0	
1	
2	
. . .	
Magnets touching	

2. Undo a second wrap, reset the magnet, and give another controlled tug. Rate it on the same scale, and record your rating across from the corresponding "number of wraps undone" number. Keep going until the magnets are touching.

3. Extra Credit: Make a graph! Graphs are really useful tools that help us visualize data like the data points you took in your table. For each number of wraps undone (these are the values on the X axis), record the "amount of force" rating you wrote down (along the Y axis).

4. Extra Credit: With your graph all done, it's time to interpret the data to figure out what it means! Start making observations. When the magnets were far apart, how big of a change in force happened by just removing one wrap? Was it a big or a small change? And how does it compare to the change in force when the magnets are almost touching? What do you think it means about how magnets work? It's all about questions now—what questions do you have about the experiment? How might you go about answering them?

5. Extra Credit: Taking it further: think about how strong these magnets are and the intensity of the fields that give them that strength. It might be enough to levitate a paper ship, which is totally cool. But how strong of a magnetic field would it take to make a football-size ship hover above the Earth with a tiny alien and a fourth-grader hanging from it? Especially really high off the ground? That's a strong magnetic force! We're going to need a lot more magnets. . . .

Space Invaders

01

The Mess I Made

It's hard to be a kid these days.

Think about it.

You've got chores, tons of homework, and little brothers. Moms and dads are always bossing you around and saying they know best. Coaches make sour faces every time you take batting practice. And teachers think learning is the most exciting thing ever invented.

It can all be a bit much for a fourth grader to handle without going nuts.

Now add to all that the responsibility of

ensuring the survival of the human race, and you get a glimpse into my life.

I've pretty much gone nutty.

And it's easy to pinpoint exactly when it all went wrong: the day Amp arrived.

Amp is the avocado-size alien who burst into my life when he flew through my window screen. His football-size spaceship dented my bedroom wall and crash-landed on my bed.

Connecting the dots from that first, shocking night to the possible end of mankind wasn't easy to do. But that didn't mean it was any less true. Because that moment so many months ago really had led directly to this night. Earth—and the billions of people living on it—was in serious crisis, even if they didn't know it yet.

Which was, more or less, what I was thinking about as I flew through the cool night in my underwear. I was clinging to Amp's spaceship for dear life as an army of soldiers chased me from below and an alien force poised to invade Earth floated above me in the starry sky.

As I said, it was an odd time for a kid whose biggest accomplishment previously had been

2

making the travel baseball team as a catcher with a pretty decent throw to second base and a so-so batting average.

Despite all that, the world was counting on me. Now if I could only find some pants.

Face-Plant

Amp landed near Olivia and her grandfather.

Or I should say, Amp dumped me off the top of his spaceship from about eight feet in the air, and I face-planted on some sharp pine needles near Olivia and her grandfather. Then Amp landed safely, all comfy cozy inside his spaceship.

Olivia and her grandfather had been waiting for us to return to make our getaway, which I now realized would be harder than we'd expected. The dark woods around us were filled with the sound of men shouting orders. Beams of light flashed through the trees. An army helicopter with a superbright searchlight roared above us.

The soldiers in the fort from which we had just escaped were coming after us. They were determined not to let us get away easily.

4

Olivia emerged out of the darkness to help me up. "Why . . . why are you wearing only your unmentionables? Wh-where are your pants?" she stammered. "And your shoes and socks and shirt?"

"Kind of hard to explain," I said, gasping and plucking off dried pine needles. I stumbled, trying to shake the dizziness. The woods spun around me. I put my hands on my knees and concentrated on not throwing up.

Olivia ran to the truck. Her grandfather was on one knee by Amp's ship. It steamed visibly and had a slight golden glow to it. It looked more futuristic out here in the woods than it had under the wool blanket in my closet, which was where it had sat, unused, for weeks.

"We've got to get out of here," Olivia said, handing me her grandfather's vest.

I zipped it up, but it was way too big. I felt like I was wearing a dress.

"Step into these," Olivia demanded, setting down huge, waterproof hunting boots.

I did as she said, and my toes searched the inside of the giant boots for warmth. I glanced down at myself and held my arms out. "I look ridiculous!"

She gave a small, nervous laugh. "You look cute." She punched me on the arm.

"Oh, brother," I said.

"They're coming," Olivia's grandfather noted, climbing into the cab of his truck through the passenger side. He had Amp's spaceship under his arm. "Let's go, you two."

Seconds later we were driving along the twisting road that ran through the woods. The helicopters were still buzzing around in the sky, so we had to drive with the headlights off. Nobody spoke. My fingers gripped the dashboard so hard, they ached.

"Is he really in there?" Olivia's grandfather said, stealing a glance down at the spaceship that now sat in Olivia's lap. "Your friend? Is he really inside that thing?"

"Yes, Grandpa," Olivia said. "You'll like him. He's weird, but he's totally harmless."

"He's normally not so shy," I said. "Honestly, he never stops jabbering. You want to meet him?"

"Not right now. Let's keep him in there, okay?" he said quietly.

"Oh, Amp kind of does what he wants when he wants," Olivia explained. "In fact, he usually does

6

exactly what you don't want him to do." She cleared her throat. "Sorry, Grandpa, for keeping Amp a secret. Zack and I decided not to tell anyone."

"We thought that would be best for everybody," I put in.

He grunted, his face pushed out over the steering wheel to better concentrate on the road.

Then Olivia's grandfather braked suddenly and peered at the woods on the right side.

"Did you see something?" I asked with alarm. "What is it?"

"A bear?" Olivia said. "A deer? Army guys? Aliens? Bigfoot?"

He shushed us and slowed the truck even more. He flipped on the parking lights, which lit the road in front of us with a dim yellow glow. I was glad to have even a little bit of light to guide us, but now we were barely moving.

"Are we running out of gas?" Olivia asked. "That would not be good timing."

"Do you have to go to the bathroom?" I asked, searching his face, which was now lit by the weak light coming from the dashboard. I could see his face was creased with focus.

I kept turning around to look down the road behind us, expecting to see army truck headlights glaring.

"Yeah, a potty break right now would be pretty lame, Grandpa," Olivia said. She turned to me. "Sometimes people Grandpa's age can't help—"

"Shush, you two," he said. We were now going about only five miles per hour. "They'll set up roadblocks at the end of this valley."

We thought about that for a moment.

"That is so intense," Olivia said quietly.

"There it is," Olivia's grandfather said with relief in his voice.

We turned slowly off the smooth main road and onto a bumpy gravel path. The truck squeaked and groaned in protest.

A dim, single lightbulb appeared out of the darkness above a cracked and faded sign that said BENNETT LAKE PARK.

I checked behind us one last time as we left the road; nobody was in hot pursuit. Yet.

"Came to fish here a few times," Olivia's grandfather said, and sighed. "Terrible fishing. Trout no bigger than your hand."

8

After a minute a locked gate appeared in front of us next to a deserted ranger station hut where people must have to pay to enter the park during fishing season. The truck turned and rolled slowly into the small dirt parking space next to the hut. We parked with most of the truck pushed into the bushes. I could hear a few twigs snap as the truck moved forward. The branches of a giant tree slapped at the top of the truck's cab and hung low over its bed. It was a good hiding place.

"Wait, is this a potty break?" Olivia asked.

"Nope," Olivia's grandfather said, turning the key and plunging us into silence.

We sat in the dark. The engine clicked and gurgled as it cooled down. I heard an owl hoot nearby.

"We are going to break into that ranger station and use it to figure out a plan."

"Isn't that illegal?" I asked.

"Oh, I imagine we've already broken a few dozen federal and state laws tonight," he said with a hint of humor in his voice.

I rubbed my chilled arms. "Do you think we're on the FBI's ten most wanted list?" I asked.

"No"—Olivia's grandfather sighed—"but the

night is still young."

"You can meet Amp when we get inside," Olivia said excitedly. "He's never really met an adult before. He is so funny."

"We also might want to discuss preventing the destruction of Earth and everyone who lives on it," I mumbled.